Mole in a hole

Lesley Sims

Illustrated by David Semple

Mole gives a groan.
His home is too small.

There's no room for me! Oh... no room at all.

"I'm not very tall,
but I need a new place...

Mole's Big
New
Home

...with trees and a view
and plenty of space."

He picks up his shovel
and sticks on his hat.

In a big open field
he starts to dig...

SPLAT!

Mole tries a new hole.
He finds acorns galore.

"Not there!" Squirrel squeaks.
"That's my secret store."

Mole tries a third time
near a hill, by three trees.

He sighs.
"All this digging is hard on my knees!"

I need a digger to make this hole bigger!

He digs up
old bowls,

boots
and roots,

sticks and
stones...

Then what does he see but ENORMOUS old bones.

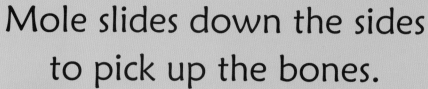

Mole slides down the sides
to pick up the bones.

What bad luck!
Mole is stuck.

He moans and
he groans.

He hooks them together

one bone...

two bones...

three...

Hooray! Mole is out.
"Just look at the mess,"
shout Rabbit and Squirrel.

You'll clean
it up? Yes?

I'll fix it
right now.

But how? Can you guess?

Mole works away until it gets dark...

Now everyone plays in

Mole's Dinosaur Park!

About phonics

Phonics is a method of teaching reading used extensively in today's schools. At its heart is an emphasis on identifying the *sounds* of letters, or combinations of letters, that are then put together to make words. These sounds are known as phonemes.

Starting to read

Learning to read is an important milestone for any child. The process can begin well before children start to learn letters and put them together to read words. The sooner children can discover books and enjoy stories and language, the better they will be prepared for reading themselves, first with the help of an adult and then independently.

You can find out more about phonics on the Usborne Very First Reading website, **www.usborne.com/veryfirstreading** (US readers go to **www.veryfirstreading.com**). Click on the **Parents** tab at the top of the page, then scroll down and click on **About synthetic phonics**.

Phonemic awareness

An important early stage in pre-reading and early reading is developing phonemic awareness: that is, listening out for the sounds within words. Rhymes, rhyming stories and alliteration are excellent ways of encouraging phonemic awareness.

In this story, your child will soon identify the *o* sound, made by the *o-e* combination, as in **mole** and **hole**. Look out, too, for rhymes such as **stones** – **bones** and **store** – **galore**.

Hearing your child read

If your child is reading a story to you, don't rush to correct mistakes, but be ready to prompt or guide if he or she is struggling. Above all, do give plenty of praise and encouragement.

Edited by Jenny Tyler
Designed by Sam Whibley

Reading consultants: Alison Kelly and Anne Washtell

First published in 2016 by Usborne Publishing Ltd., Usborne House, 83-85 Saffron Hill, London EC1N 8RT, England.
www.usborne.com Copyright © 2016 Usborne Publishing Ltd.